When Arthur Wouldn't Sleep

Written and illustrated by

Joseph Theobald

Collins

"Come ON, Flora," Arthur said. "Let's play jumping."

"Ssssh!" Flora mumbled. "It's bedtime. Time to go to sleep."

2

The butterflies weren't sleeping, the bees were busy
buzzing and the grasshoppers were jumping all over
the place.

"I don't want to go to sleep," grumbled Arthur.

Arthur gazed up at the clouds.

The more he gazed, the more funny shapes he saw.

Then he started feeling very light.

Slowly, he started going up and up and UP.

5

Soon he met a hippo.

"Where do you want to go?" the hippo asked.

"I want to go where no one goes to sleep," Arthur said.

And off they flew.

"This is your stop," said the hippo.
A ladybird was waiting for Arthur.

"Come with me," said the ladybird. "But don't forget.
No sleeping!"

Soon they arrived at a party.
What a party!

"It's time for the Amazing Crazylegs Dancing
Competition," the grasshopper said.

10

They danced and jumped ...
Arthur joined in too.

The ladybird bounced, the sheep pranced and the grasshopper skipped and hopped and twirled.

14

They jumped and danced ... until their legs felt like jelly and they couldn't dance another step.

Who was going to win the Amazing Crazylegs Dancing Competition?

15

The grasshopper said, "... and the winner is ...
ARTHUR! Do another dance, Arthur!"

But Arthur was very sleepy.
"I have to go now," he said. "I've got to tell Flora
that there's a place where no one goes to sleep."

Off he flew, over the fields and back to Flora.

But Arthur didn't tell Flora about the place where no one goes to sleep ...

18

19

... because in the morning, he'd forgotten all about it.

20

21

Have you been
where no one goes to sleep?
It's out of this world!
Fly there by hippo.
Meet new friends: the ladybird,
the grasshopper and the dancing sheep.
Listen to the Amazing Crazylegs Dance Band.
Dance in the
Amazing Crazylegs
Dancing Competition!

Don't forget:
no sleeping!

# Ideas for reading

Written by Clare Dowdall BA(Ed), MA(Ed)
Lecturer and Primary Literacy Consultant

Learning objectives: read longer phrases and more complex sentences; search for and use familiar syllables within words to read longer words; attend to a greater range of punctuation and text layout; read aloud with intonation and expression appropriate to the grammar and punctuation; predict story endings/incidents; speak with clarity and intonation when reading and reciting texts

Curriculum links: Citizenship: Choices, living in a diverse world; PSHE: feelings

Interest words: mumbled, grumbled, butterflies, grasshoppers, gazed, hippo, ladybird, Crazylegs, competition, pranced, twirled

Word count: 280

Getting started

- Introduce the story to the children by sharing the blurb. Discuss the question – *Where could Arthur go?*

- Read the title together and ask the children to share their own experiences of not being able or willing to sleep. *How does it feel when this happens?* Explain that Arthur, the main character in this story, feels grumpy about it.

- Read up to and including p3 where Arthur grumbles his speech. Experiment with reading this aloud with good expression and characterisation, paying attention to the punctuation.

- Skim through the pages up to p21, and ask the children to follow what is happening in the pictures, and how Arthur is feeling at each point.

Reading and responding

- Ask the children to read independently and quietly to p21. Observe their progress and praise good expression and intonation.

- Before turning each page, ask the children to predict what might happen next. As the story progresses, can they predict how it might end?